# Do you still love me?

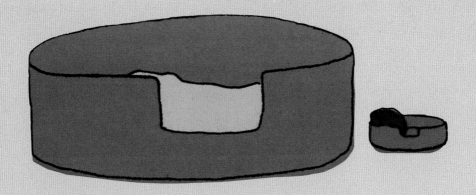

# For Grandma
## – Charlotte

First published in 2002 in Great Britain
by Gullane Children's Books
This edition first published in 2002 by

## Gullane Children's Books

185 Fleet Street, London EC4A 2HS
www.gullanebooks.com

10   9   8   7   6   5   4   3

Text and illustrations © Charlotte Middleton 2002

The right of Charlotte Middleton to be identified as the author
and illustrator of this work has been asserted by her in
accordance with the Copyright, Designs, and Patents Act 1988.

A CIP record for this title is available from the British Library.

ISBN 978-1-86233-492-2

Printed and bound in China

Charlotte Middleton

# Do you still love me?

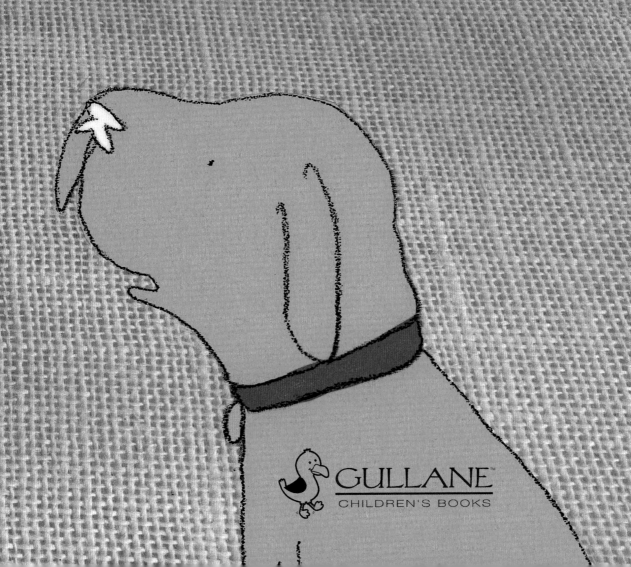

GULLANE™
CHILDREN'S BOOKS

Every day,
Dudley liked to wake up early.

And every day, he ate a hearty breakfast.

Dudley's favourite game was hide-and-seek.

He liked to impress Aunt Prym with his fleas.

BARK!

**But most of all,**

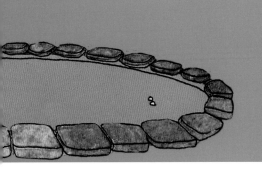

**Dudley liked scaring Gemma,**

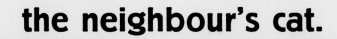 **the neighbour's cat.**

Every evening,
Dudley curled up with Anna
in their favourite place.

**Then one day, Anna brought home someone new. It was a baby chameleon, called Pequito. From then on, things weren't the same.**

Pequito always got up
even earlier than Dudley...

so Anna
was already up.

Pequito could catch his own breakfast.

Pequito
was better at
hide-and-seek.

Pequito was better at impressing Aunt Prym
although he didn't have fleas.

**All of Anna's friends were fascinated by Pequito's funny eyes.**

And no one noticed Dudley.

Chameleons have very long tongues (sometimes longer than their bodies). They use their tongues to catch insects to eat.

They usually live in warm places like deserts and rainforests.

Some make their homes on the ground; some live in trees or bushes. They are very good climbers.

And at the end of the day,
there was somebody else
in Dudley's favourite place.

Dudley felt really sad.
Pequito was better at everything and
nobody seemed to care about Dudley any more.

Later on,
when Dudley woke up,
Pequito was gone.

Dudley was glad.

But when Pequito
didn't come back,
Dudley began to get worried.

Dudley thought he had better

look for him . . .

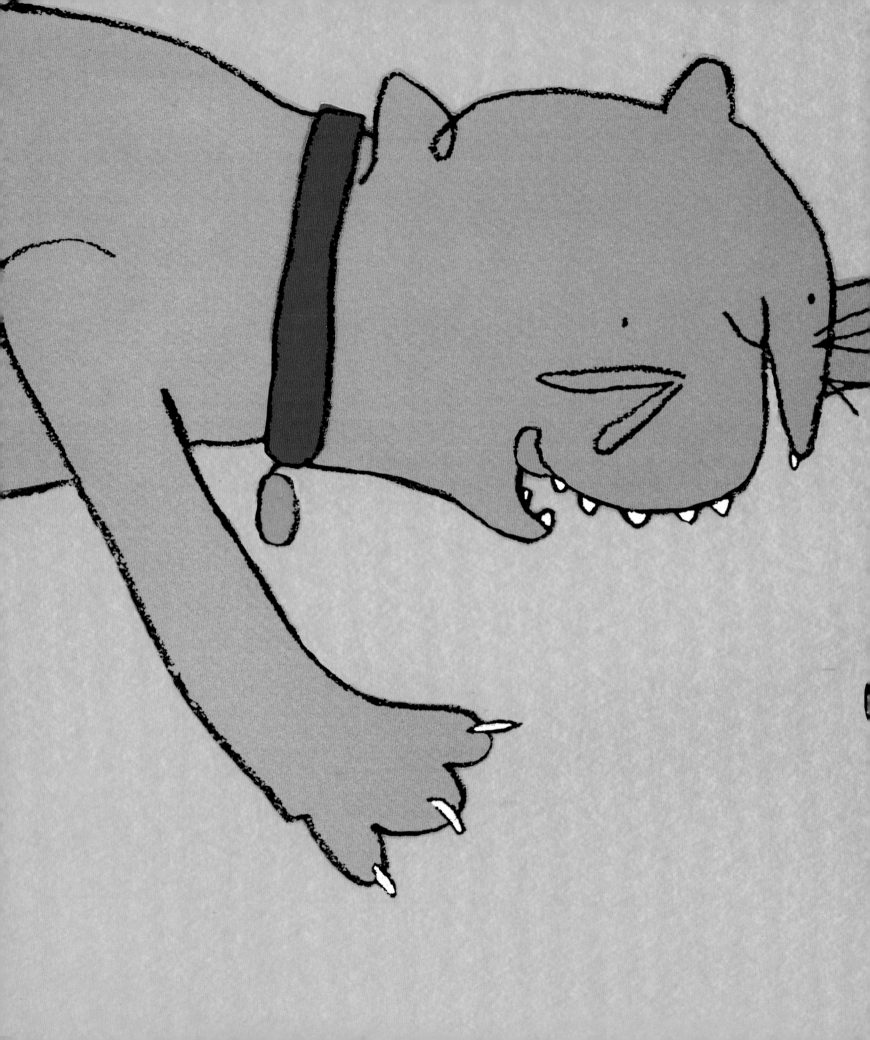

But somebody else
had already found Pequito.

Dudley barked louder
than he had ever barked before.

Anna and Pequito thought
Dudley was a **hero!**

# Giraffes

are the tallest animals on land, between 4 and 5 m tall. Their necks are over 2 m long and used for reaching up to eat leaves from trees.

Giraffes are found only in Africa, on savannahs and grassland.

They mostly live in groups. Every giraffe's coat has a unique pattern of brown spots or patches. Giraffes almost always sleep standing up.

**From then on,
Dudley spent a lot of time
doing something he was REALLY good at...**

**Looking after Pequito.**